Don't Kick Up a Fuss, Gus!

Adria Meserve

Pi don

Gus was a little zebra who lived in Africa. He loved to gallop and jump about on the hot, dusty savannah.

One morning Gus was playing.
It hadn't rained for ages so
the ground was very dry.

He stamped his hooves,

he reared,

he bucked . . .

and made the BIGGEST dust clouds ever!

Just then Mum called Gus. "Come along dear! We're going on a long walk."

"But I want to make dust clouds," said Gus, digging in his hooves.

"Don't kick up a fuss, Gus!" said Dad. "It's too hot here. The grass is dry and tough and the river has nearly dried up."

Before Gus could say anything more, his family had trotted off to join the rest of the herd.

They walked along a riverbank and through a forest.

"Walking is boring," moaned Gus. "I want to go home."
Gus's family did their best to make the journey fun.

When Gus got bored of singing, Grandma played I Spy.
"Are we nearly there yet?" asked Gus.

"Walk nose to tail," Mum told Gus.
"No galloping off on your own!" said Dad.

Dad sang Five Little Zebras with Gus,
and Mum sang Here We Go Round the Acacia Tree.

"We're much closer," said Grandpa.
"Let's play Count the Mongooses."

But then they got stuck in a traffic jam.
They waited and waited and waited to cross a bridge.

Gus got really fed up.
"Don't kick up a fuss, Gus!"
Dad said. "There's nothing
we can do."

When they finally reached
the other side of the bridge,
Gus bolted.

He leapt between a giraffe's legs,

over an elephant's trunk

and galloped out of sight.

Gus's family were furious when they
finally caught up with him.
"We're going to finish this walk
even if we have to carry you," said Dad.
"Don't kick up a fuss, Gus!"

But Gus wasn't going to give in just yet.

He kicked up

the biggest

fuss

ever!

Eventually Gus wore himself out.
"If you've quite finished we'll carry on,"
said Dad. "We need to catch up with the others."

Mum gently pushed Gus along as they
continued on their journey.
"No more fussing," she said.

At last they stopped and rested for the night. "It will all seem better in the morning," said Mum, nuzzling his mane.

The next day they made better progress.

They crossed a river,

and finally reached the top of a ridge.

Gus knew there was no point in kicking up a fuss.

trekked up and down a mountain . . .

From there they could see a lush green valley before them.
"We're nearly there!" cried Mum and pointed at
something glistening in the distance.

Gus joined the other
zebras as they bounded
down the hill, leapt off
the grassy bank and
landed in . . .

. . . THE WATERHOLE!

Gus thought it was wonderful!
He hoped he'd never have to
leave this place.

Gus jumped off rocks, dived into plunge pools and swooshed down waterfalls. He made the biggest waves ever! "We're all getting wet!" cried Gus's dad.

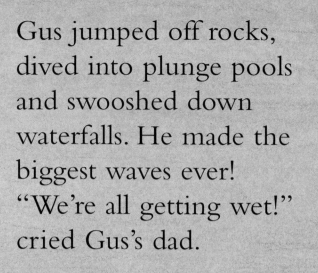

Sploosh!

"DON'T KICK UP A FUSS!"
shouted Gus, laughing.

For my lovely Isabelle

First published in Great Britain in 2009 by
Piccadilly Press Ltd, 5 Castle Road, London NW1 8PR
www.piccadillypress.co.uk

Text and illustration copyright © Adria Meserve, 2009

Designed by Simon Davis
Printed and bound in China by WKT
Colour reproduction by Dot Gradations

ISBN: 978 1 84812 012 9 (hardback)
978 1 84812 011 2 (paperback)

1 3 5 7 9 10 8 6 4 2